Big Guy

Robin Stevenson

orca soundings

Orca Book Publishers

c.1

Library and Archives Canada Cataloguing in Publication

Stevenson, Robin H. (Robin Hjordis), 1968-

Big guy / written by Robin Stevenson.
(Orca soundings)

ISBN 978-1-55143-912-9 (bound)--ISBN 978-1-55143-910-5 (pbk.)

I. Title. II. Series.
PS8637.T487B52 2008   jC813'.6   C2008-900186-9

Summary: Derek thinks he might be falling in love for the first time ever.
The problem is, he hasn't been entirely honest with his online boyfriend.

First published in the United States, 2008
Library of Congress Control Number: 2008920123

Orca Book Publishers gratefully acknowledges the support for its publishing
programs provided by the following agencies: the Government of Canada
through the Book Publishing Industry Development Program and the Canada
Council for the Arts, and the Province of British Columbia through the BC
Arts Council and the Book Publishing Tax Credit.

Cover design by Teresa Bubela
Cover photography by Getty Images
Author photo by David Lowes

Orca Book Publishers
PO Box 5626, Station B
Victoria, BC Canada
V8R 6S4

Orca Book Publishers
PO Box 468
Custer, WA USA
98240-0468

www.orcabook.com
Printed and bound in Canada.
Printed on 100% PCW recycled paper.

11 10 09 08 • 5 4 3 2 1

To Katrina and Toby, with love.

Chapter One

I'm whistling as I walk in the door, still buzzing from finding out I got the job. It's the only decent thing that's happened in months. Well—that, and meeting Ethan.

I haven't told Dad about either one.

He's home, but something seems odd. It takes me a moment to realize: the house is too quiet. For once, Dad hasn't turned on the television. Instead, he's standing staring at a picture on the wall of the three of us: himself, Mom and me.

I'm trying to decide whether to say hello or just sneak past when he turns. "Derek."

"Hi, Dad." I start to edge by, wanting to get to my computer.

He nods at the picture. "You still think about her?"

I stare at him. We don't talk about Mom. I nod, warily. "Sure. Sometimes."

"She'll be back," he says. "It's only been a couple months. She's been gone longer than that before."

"Sure, Dad," I say. *No, you idiot. It's been a year, she hates you, she's off chanting mantras with a bunch of orange-clad cult freaks in California.* I look around for a glass or bottle, wondering if he's been drinking.

He glares at me. "What do you know about it?"

"Nothing," I say. I miss her like hell, but I half hope she doesn't come back. At least one of us got away.

I slip past him and into my room, turn on the computer. *Ethan*, I think. And my heart speeds up, dances in my chest. He sent me a picture of himself a few days ago. I keep it under the mouse pad in case Dad snoops in my room. While the computer boots up, I slide it out and study it carefully, even though by now I can see it with my eyes closed.

Brown eyes, olive skin, straight dark eyebrows and an easy white-toothed grin. He's hot. I know I'm biased, but he really is. Even Gabi thinks so.

Yes! He's online.

> *hey ethan*
> *about time you got home*
> *yeah. what's up?*
> *missed u today*

I grin. I probably look like an idiot, sitting here by myself at the computer with this big grin on my face, but I can't help it. My fingers fly over the keyboard.

> *missed you too*
> *at least you have a picture of me. hint hint*

My grin freezes on my face. I was half hoping he'd forget. But to be honest, I knew he wouldn't. So I'm ready. I've been waiting.

> *sorry. keep forgetting to send one.*
> *here u go*

It's my favorite picture. My friend Gabi took it and I actually look pretty good in it. I'm leaning against the brick wall of the high school, wearing jeans, black T-shirt, leather jacket. My expression is kind of serious and my hair's a bit shorter than it is now. I'm squinting just a little and the sun is on my face. I've always been tall, always looked older than my age. I study the picture, wondering what Ethan will think.

My fingers pause, hover over the keyboard. Last chance to change my mind.

Then I send the picture.

Ethan is still chatting away, saying I look just how he imagined, but somehow I don't feel like talking anymore.

I type a quick reply, make an excuse.

> *eth? dad's yelling something. gtg.*

I log out and walk down the hall to the bathroom. I slide the dead bolt, locking the door behind me. Slowly, I pull my black T-shirt off over my head and stare at the reflection in the mirror. Rolls of fat, white slabs of blubber and misery. I grab fistfuls of it, dig my fingernails in hard enough to leave sharp red crescent-shaped marks.

That picture I sent? It was taken last year, before Mom left. Before I packed on all this fat. That was a good eighty pounds ago. You wouldn't even recognize me if you saw me now.

I barely recognize myself.

Chapter Two

Since ninth grade, I've bagged groceries after school, down at the A & P. I don't know why, exactly, but when I dropped out of school a few months back, I felt like I should do something different. Move on, you know? Plus, the pay was pretty crappy. But now, first day of the new job, I'm wishing I was back at the A & P with the rest of the guys.

To be honest, this job's a little freaky. I thought I could do it, but now I'm not so sure.

I'm standing in the middle of the living room in one of the residents' apartments. It's bigger than I expected. It's a large square room with a gray carpet, not much furniture, a narrow window overlooking a parking lot.

I glance down at my file and read her name again. Aaliyah Manon. I don't have a clue how to say it. I should've paid more attention during the orientation. I dredge through the mud of my memory and come up with an image of Francine's mouth opening and closing as she drones on and on. I can remember her smoker's breath and the way her red lipstick bled into the little wrinkles around her mouth, but I can't remember anything that's going to help me get through this next hour.

"Hello?" I call out.

No answer.

I cross the living room and gaze out the window. Eight in the morning and barely light out. Pouring rain. It's rained every freaking day this month. Cars pull in and out of the parking lot, an occasional pedestrian hurries by, clutching an umbrella. Above the street, red brick buildings meet a greasy gray sky.

I look at my watch. My stomach is a tight twisting knot.

"In a rush, are you?" a voice says.

I look up, wondering how she managed to enter the living room so quietly in that bulky wheelchair. The first thing that strikes me is how young she is. Not more than thirty. Maybe even younger. I'm surprised. Francine told me most of the residents were old. The woman is very thin, and one side of her face is pulled downward, mouth and eye drooping slightly. It makes her expression hard to read.

"I told them not to send a guy," she says. "Francine knows I don't like male care workers." Her speech is slurred, but despite this her voice has a sharp edge that adds to my nervousness.

"I'm sorry," I say. "Do you want me to call Francine? See if there is someone else?"

She shakes her head. "No," she says. "I have to be somewhere in an hour. I need to get ready."

"Okay then." I think back to Francine's words this morning. Just be matter-of-fact, Francine said. Remember, the residents are used to having assistance with personal care. If you aren't sure about something, ask.

"What can I help you with, then?" I realize I've forgotten to introduce myself. "Ahh…I'm Derek."

Aaliyah struggles to push her long dark hair off her face. Her movements are stiff and jerky. "I need to shower. I need help washing my hair and getting dressed."

"No problem," I say. I manage to keep my voice light, but inside I'm freaking out a little. I'd take my old job back, right now, if I had the chance. Screw the three-dollars-an-hour pay difference. I dig my fingernails into my palm and follow the wheelchair down the hallway.

The bathroom is large and a sling hangs from the ceiling.

Aaliyah sees me looking at it. "I'm not using that anymore," she says. "You just have to help me move onto the chair."

Chair? Then I see it, in the shower: a

plastic chair with little holes in it for the water to run through. "Okay."

She sighs. "Are you new? I mean, I know you're new here, but please tell me you've done this before."

Here's the thing: I had to lie a little to get hired. Okay, more than a little. I told them I was twenty and that I'd done a couple of college courses. Told them I took care of my aunt who has MS. No one ever checks up on stuff like that. Truth is, I'm seventeen, just dropped out of high school, don't even have an aunt.

I shrug. "I've, ahhh, done some…"

Aaliyah's eyes are scalpel-sharp and I look away. "No. Ahhh…no, I'm new."

"Damn it," she says. Francine warned me that some of the residents could be difficult. Just stay calm, she said. Talk slowly. Be aware that you may have to repeat the same information several times.

Repeating that I'm new doesn't seem like a good idea.

Aaliyah sighs. "Sorry," she says.

I don't meet her eyes. "Shall I…"

"Yes. Help me get undressed."

She is wearing flannel pyjamas, blue with a pattern of soft yellow flowers. I undo the small pearl buttons with cold fingers and try to slip the top down over her shoulders. It's not so easy freeing her stiff arms from the sleeves. She's really skinny, and I'm clumsy and awkward and scared of hurting her. At last the pyjama top comes away in my hands. Aaliyah sits half naked in her wheelchair, her arms folded across her chest. I look away, my neck and cheeks flaming.

I can't think how to take the pants off with her sitting down. I remember her saying she hated having male care workers, and I wonder if she'd feel any better if she knew I was gay. Maybe I should tell her. Then again, maybe not. Who knows what she'd think?

Aaliyah gestures for me to come closer. "Look, you have turn on the shower, let it warm up. Then you have to help me up. I can walk a couple of steps, with support. Help me get the pants off and transfer to the chair."

I nod numbly, turn on the shower and hold my hand under the spray until it runs warm.

I turn back to Aaliyah, put one arm around her back. Her shoulder blades jut out. Bird bones. Her spine is a chain of sharp bumps. She flinches and shivers, skin jumping, and I realize that my sleeve is wet from the shower and has dripped water down her back.

"Sorry," I say under my breath.

She ignores me. Her forehead is creased in concentration as she struggles to stand. She weighs almost nothing and, despite my clumsiness, it isn't all that difficult to remove her pants, help her into the shower and lower her onto the chair.

In the shower, Aaliyah closes her eyes and turns her face into the spray. Water streams from her dark hair, over her shoulders and breasts. I look away again, embarrassed. My reflection stares back at me from the bathroom mirror: tall and dark but a solid eighty pounds past handsome. As always, my appearance shocks me. Disgusts me. Even after a year of getting steadily fatter, this still isn't how I see myself.

Aaliyah's voice startles me. "I haven't always been like this," she says.

For a second I think she's reading my mind. Then it sinks in that she's talking about herself. I just nod. I mean, what am I supposed to say to that? Me neither? I sneak a sideways peek at her and realize she can't see me nodding anyway. Her eyes are closed.

I glance in the mirror again, remembering the photo I sent Ethan. My stomach twists a little.

I never wanted to lie to him. But what choice did I have?

Chapter Three

I grab the shampoo and pour some on my hands, rub her thick wet hair between my fingers. I snag a tangle and Aaliyah jerks her head away.

"Sorry," I mutter.

I've used too much shampoo and it takes me ages to rinse it all off. Neither of us talk. Finally I am drying her off and she sits, towel-wrapped, in her wheelchair.

When she finally looks at me, her eyes are dark and unreadable. It's like she just put on a pair of sunglasses, like she's closed herself off, and if I look at her, I'm just going to see my own reflection.

"Get my clothes from the bedroom," she says. "I need to get dressed."

Her bedroom is painted blue, with ruffled bedsheets and brightly colored paintings on the walls. A photograph on the dresser catches my eye. It's a picture of a girl standing on the deck of a sailboat, one hand raised to catch the long dark hair blowing across her face. She's leaning back against a man who stands behind her, arms wrapped tightly round her waist. She is laughing, mouth slightly open, eyes crinkled. It's her. Aaliyah.

"They're on my bed," she calls.

I pull my eyes away from the photograph and retrace my steps back down the hall. "Yeah. I found them."

The whole time I'm helping her dress, I'm wondering what happened to her. Like, does she have some disease or illness or something? Or was she in some kind of accident? I flex my muscles slightly, bend my knees. It makes me feel weird, thinking about it. To be honest, I can't get out of her apartment fast enough. I can't wait to get home and talk to Ethan.

So what if I sent an old photo. It's no big deal. It's still me, just a thinner version. And just thinking about him, I can feel the corners of my mouth twitching in a stupid happy grin.

Being in love is way better than any drug out there.

The rest of the day is all right, I guess. I help a couple of other residents get dressed, brush their teeth, whatever. They're all in their seventies and eighties. Old people. Some of them are kind of out of it. Some seem pretty okay and show me pictures of their grandkids. Some are grumpy as hell. Whatever. I help feed some old guy who complains a lot. I water plants. I even clean a freaking goldfish tank for one old lady.

At the end of the day, Francine catches me in the hall. She is wearing a peach-colored dress, too tight in the hips. It's one of those pastel colors nurses always wear in hospitals, and she has on those white nurse shoes too. I figure maybe she wants people to think she really is a nurse.

"Derek. How was your first day?" She stands in front of me, blocking my path.

I shrug. "Fine."

She tilts her head to one side, forehead creasing. "No questions?"

"No. No questions," I say.

Outside, it is still raining hard. Four o'clock and already starting to get dark. This November it seems like the sun can hardly be bothered to come up at all. Like it takes too much effort for the sun to rise when it's just going to have to set again in a few hours, and no one is going to see it through the clouds anyway.

I drive home. Dad's not home, which is fine by me. I'm not in the mood for another talk about how I could get a girlfriend more easily if I'd just lose a few pounds, blah blah blah. I stand at the fridge and eat leftover pasta straight out of the plastic container.

Then, like I do practically every night, I head to the computer.

My dad hates this. He'd like me to be out playing football or hockey, even though all he does is sit on the couch and drink beer. Dad likes to give advice on things he's clueless about. "Time you had a relationship," he said the other day. "It's not healthy, spending all your time on the computer." Hah. He thinks he's the expert on relationships. Sure, he slapped me and Mom around, but he watches the *Dr. Phil* show religiously.

Jerk.

But I'm not stupid. I do actually realize that most people have relationships. You know, with real live people who they actually meet. It's just not so easy when you're living in a small town, you're seventeen and you're queer.

Not to mention fat.

Anyway, there are maybe four hundred students in my high school. If that ten percent figure people are always quoting is true, forty of them should be queer. Other than me, I only know one for sure, and that's Gabi, my best friend since first grade.

So Ethan and I may only talk online, but it's no less real for that. He lives out west and we've been talking, on and off, for a few months now. Some people might think that's kind of pathetic, you know, online dating, but it's actually been really intense. It's like this dance we've been doing, getting to know each other, kind of flirting I guess, but becoming friends too.

More than friends.

To tell you the truth, I'm pretty crazy about this guy. Did I already mention that?

I log on to MSN and there's a message from Ethan.

> *hey derek. i'm at work—booorrrrring.
> boss keeps hanging around so can't
> surf. might actually have to work if u
> don't get home soon, lol*

I grin. Ethan's working part-time as a research assistant, inputting data for one of his mother's professor friends. He's doing grade twelve too—he thinks I should go back and finish, but I'd had enough.

> *hey,* I type. *just got home.
> how was first day?*

I think for a minute. Then I type

> *definitely weird.*
>
> *tell me more*

I love this about Ethan—he's really interested in stuff. I mean, everyone would ask how your first day was, but it's just to be polite. Not Ethan. He really wants to know.

> *th boss francine is scary nurse-type*
> *with those scary white shoes, u no?*
> *lol. and?*
> *a lot of lipstick*
> *ha ha. i mean what did u do?*
> *i helped some lady have a shower*
> *u didn't*
> *did*
> *yeah that'd be weird*

I feel a twinge of guilt talking about Aaliyah like this, but I push it aside. Another message pops up from Ethan.

> *derek—gtg*

And he's gone. Just gotta go. Not *love ya* or *later babe* or even *L8R G8R*. Nothing remotely affectionate. Instantly my insides are tight and squirming and I'm wondering what's wrong. Maybe he was just in a hurry.

Maybe his boss walked in. And he messaged me to find out how my first day was. He wouldn't do that if he was about to dump me, right? If he was losing interest?

I hate this. I hate how one stupid little conversation that isn't even about anything can send me over the edge and turn me into a stupid fat seething mass of insecurity. Before Ethan, I was fine. Eternally single, maybe, but fine. I had friends. I wasn't on the edge of panic over a missing word.

The thing is, even though it's all online and it's only been a few months, it's already kind of hard to imagine my life without Ethan in it.

Chapter Four

I'm still sitting there, staring at the screen, when another message pops up.

u still there?

yup, still here.

I rub my hands over my face, relieved and a bit embarrassed. God, I'm glad Ethan has no idea how pathetic I am. Has no idea how crazy in love with him I am.

my mom just phoned and guess what?

I shake my head. Here I am panicking and he was just talking to his mom.

ok what?

i have amazing news…

I'm grinning as I type.

u r such a tease. what news?

my sister's getting married in february…

woo hoo

wait, this is good. th weddings in kitchener. that's close to you rite?

I'm grinning so hard it hurts. I feel like my heart might explode.

hell yeah. like a half hr drive

we're gonna actually MIRL

Meet in real life. My fingers are flying over the keys.

brilliant. can't believe it

me neither

To actually be able to see Ethan, to meet him, to touch him and hold him and…

And my heart practically thuds to a halt in my chest as I remember.

That photo I sent him. That's who he thinks I am. That's who he wants to meet. Not me. Not this version of me.

I can't meet him.

I sit for a few minutes, just staring at the screen. A message pops up.

> *u still there?*

I know what I need to say:

> *Ethan, I don't think that's a good idea. In fact, I've been thinking maybe we should just forget about the whole thing—*but I can't.

I can't do it.

I can't bring myself to end it yet, even though I know I will have to.

I start typing.

> *yeah still here. just surprised. wow*
>
> *u sure? u wondering if I'm really a creepy 40 yr old perv?*

I wish that was what I was worrying about.

> *no I googled u months ago. found your soccer team picture from 10th grade remember?*
>
> *uh huh. i look better now*
>
> *can't wait to see u*
>
> *and? wink wink*
>
> *yeah that too*

I am grinning again, playing around, almost forgetting for a moment that none of this is going to happen. Then it hits me again like a wall of ice, hard and cold and inevitable. God.

I can't tell him not to come. I can't do it.

And I know I don't have a choice.

I stare at the computer for a few seconds, trying to find it in me to keep chatting and goofing around like everything is okay. Like nothing is wrong.

The front door opens and slams closed.

ethan? I type, my fingers suddenly slow and awkward on the keyboard. *dad's home. ttyl*

I grab my leather jacket off the back of my door, check that my car keys are in the pocket. Time to go.

Dad glares at me as I walk by. "Where are you going?"

"Out."

He snorts, turns on the television and sits down on the couch. Conversation over. He's never been a big talker, but since Mom took off it's like he's forgotten how. Fine by me. When he does talk, it's usually just to give me a lecture.

Down at the bar—the only one in town—I see some of the guys I went to school with. Mason and Todd. We used to work together at the A & P.

"Hey hey," Mason drawls, lifting one hand in a mock salute. His red hair is buzzed short, his large nose still red from a bad sunburn a few months back. "Come and join us, big guy."

I shrug. "Yeah, okay." Everyone's called me that since about sixth grade. I've always been tall. Since I got fat, though, I've started to hate that nickname. I slap some money down on the bar and carry a pint over to their table. Technically, I'm underage, but no one ever gets ID'd here.

Todd's girlfriend is with them. Carrie. She's tiny and sharp-featured. With her puffed-up hair and startled brown eyes she looks like one of those toy poodles.

She loops her arm through Todd's and smiles up at me. "Hey, Derek."

Todd puts his beer down and looks at me, thick eyebrows raised. "So," he says, "I hear you got a new job."

"Yeah."

"And?"

I shrug. "It's okay."

"Okay? You give up a chance to bag groceries with us for a job that's just okay?" His skinny face is creased with laughter. "Come on. What do you have to do? Help people with Old-Timer's find the dining room?"

I nod, take a long drink of cold beer. "Yeah, basically." I glance around and my eyes fall on the pool table. I dig in my pocket and come up with a dollar. "Who's up for a game?"

The evening passes in a blur of jukebox oldies, rounds of beer, games of pool won and lost. Thoughts are bouncing around in my head: Ethan. That photo I sent. His plan to visit. And that woman, Aaliyah—I keep thinking about her too, wondering what happened to her. I order another beer and push the thoughts aside. When we finally stagger out into the rain, it's past midnight. A river of brown water rushes along the gutter and I swear aloud as I step in it, soaking my foot to the ankle as I fumble to find my car keys.

"You sure you're okay to drive?" Todd asks me.

"Fine," I say.

Todd looks worried and glances at Carrie, who is clinging wetly to his arm. "I didn't realize you had your car, man. You had a lot to drink. I mean, you know, you don't usually…"

I sit down heavily in the driver's seat, start the car, flick on the wipers. "It's cool. I'm fine. Give you guys a ride if you want."

Todd looks at me, brow furrowed. Then he looks back at Carrie. "No, we're good, we'll get a cab." He waves. "All right, big guy. See you."

I head straight down King Street, through downtown. Traffic is a snarled mess. Half the streetlights aren't working, and power seems to be out in some parts of town. I turn on the radio, sing along to an old Rolling Stones song, my voice loud and out of tune, joining Mick Jagger's as he belts out "Paint It Black."

I'm just turning onto Walnut Street when a pickup truck cuts me off, veering sharply into my lane. I hit the brakes hard. The car swerves and starts to skid. I'm drunk, I think. I take my foot off the brakes and wrestle the car back under control. I pull to a careful stop at the side of the road. I'm shaking all over, sitting with my head against the steering wheel. God.

Mick Jagger just keeps on singing. I open the door and puke my guts into the gutter. Then I leave the car at the side of the road and walk the last two miles home.

Chapter Five

The next day I oversleep. I have to catch a bus to pick up my car. Don't even have time to go online. I show up at work twenty minutes late, with a jackhammer headache and a stomach full of acid.

Francine greets me coldly. She is wearing mint green today. Her thin blond hair is pulled back tightly, penciled-on eyebrows arching above eye shadow the same color as her dress.

"You're with Mrs. Buckley this morning,"

she says, dropping a stack of papers on her desk but not sitting down. "Cleaning. She's been hiding food again and her unit stinks to high heaven."

My stomach rolls in protest at the thought. "And after that?"

"We'll need help in the dining room. We're short-staffed." She lifts her chin and, despite being about a foot shorter, somehow manages to look down her nose at me. "I should remind you, Derek, that you are on a probationary period. Further lateness will not be tolerated."

"Sorry," I mutter.

I spend a couple of hours picking moldy bits of food out of Mrs. Buckley's radiators and dresser drawers, and wondering if Aaliyah told Francine that she didn't want to see me again.

Mrs. Buckley keeps complaining that I'm trying to starve her.

"You're just like all the others," she says bitterly. "Everyone wants to get rid of me." Her faded blue eyes brim with tears.

The desire to defend myself flickers and dies. We sit in silence for a moment, contemplating half a bagel sticking out from beneath a pile of clothes.

"Mrs. Buckley," I say tentatively.

She looks startled, as if she had already forgotten that I was there. "Yes, dear."

"Would you mind, I mean, would it be okay if I just ran out for a couple of minutes? To talk to someone?"

She pats her white curly hair. "Of course. I'll be just fine."

I wonder if she'll take all the food out of the garbage bag and hide it again as soon as I leave the room. "Thanks."

Out in the hallway, I hesitate. Jesus Christ. What am I doing? But here I am, walking down the hall, knocking quietly on Aaliyah's door and hoping Francine doesn't come by and see me.

"Come in," Aaliyah calls.

I open her door and slip inside, walk down the hallway to her bedroom. She is still in her pyjamas, lying on her bed reading a book. When I walk in, she puts the book down and stares at me.

"You again."

I shrug. "I'm not supposed to, I mean, I'm not here to help you today." I wince at my choice of words. "I mean, Francine didn't tell me to come."

She just waits.

I turn away and put my hand on the blinds. "You want these open?"

"Yes."

I yank on the cord, pull the blinds up. Outside, the rain pours down.

"It's the twenty-seventh consecutive day of rain," Aaliyah says from behind me. "If it rains for two more, it'll be a record."

I turn slowly back toward her and rest one hand on the edge of her bed. "I'm sorry," I say. "About yesterday."

She looks at me steadily.

"When you said you hadn't always been… you know."

Aaliyah shifts her head on her pillow. "Disabled?"

"Yeah. And I didn't say anything."

"Yes."

There is a long silence. I look over at the

dresser but the photograph is gone. "I saw the photo. On the boat."

"*Carpe Diem*," she says. She laughs. "There's a certain irony in that, I suppose."

"Huh?"

She gives a short laugh. "Her name. The boat. My fiancé's boat."

I'm still staring at her blankly and she shrugs, sighs. "It means seize the day."

I meet her eyes. "Your fiancé. That was him in the picture?"

"Yes."

"What…" I falter.

"You want to know what happened? With my fiancé or to me?"

I've never noticed before, but she's got these amazing dark eyes. "To you."

She studies me. "How come you want to know now?"

I hesitate. "I don't know. I just…I can't stop thinking about it." I shake my head, my cheeks hot. "It's none of my business. I'm sorry. I don't know what I'm doing here."

She just keeps looking at me and there's something like pity on her face.

I stand up and back away slowly. "I'm sorry. I'll go. I just, you know, I didn't expect to see someone young here. I mean, it makes you think, you know? Like…I totally could have crashed my car last night. And I just thought…"

She looks past me, out the window. Her voice is like glass: sharp, fragile, cutting. "You want to know what happened to me. You want to hear that I did something stupid. So you can go on feeling like you're going to be fine. Like it would never happen to you. Like you're safe."

Outside, the rain pours down. It fills the gutters, streams from the corners of roofs, overflows the puddles in the parking lot below. I want to tell her she's wrong, that's not what I meant, but I don't say anything. I close my eyes, see blackness, feel my heart thudding wildly.

"You'll have to figure out your own life," she says, "I've got enough to deal with. Nothing personal, but I don't need your crap to deal with too."

Chapter Six

When I leave work at 4 PM, the rain is still sluicing down. I walk out the door and stand in the parking lot for a few minutes, letting the cool water stream down my face, over my shoulders, down my back. If Aaliyah was looking out her window, she'd see me standing down here like a big fat idiot. I shake my head, water flying from my too-long hair, and get in my car.

I log on at our usual time, almost without

thinking about it. Almost forgetting, again, that I have to end this. To tell you the truth, it's kind of weird how easy it is just to pretend that everything is fine.

Until Ethan's message pops up on the screen.

> *hey there cutie. i printed ur pic and now i can look at you while we talk.*

I feel sick. It's just starting to sink in: I've wrecked everything. Wrecked the one really good thing in my life. Even if the wedding got cancelled, even if Ethan decided not to visit after all…somehow I don't think things could go back to being the way they were. Not for me. I feel like I'm just faking it all now, like I'm pretending to be someone else.

And the worst part is, other than Gabi, Ethan was the only person I could be myself with. Now that's gone.

So I lie, which is something that living with my dad teaches you to do pretty well.

> *hey ethan. dont let my good looks distract u from my witty and intelligent words*

no chance. well...sorry, what were u saying?
ROFL.

I almost smile despite myself. Rolling on the floor laughing.

It couldn't be further from the truth.

The next day I show up to work on time. Francine gives me a curt nod.

"Well, I don't know what you did, but you sure charmed Mrs. Buckley yesterday."

"I did?"

"Mmm-hmm." Francine's red painted lips stretch thin as she smiles at me. "So I thought you could do her bath this morning. She's been giving Paula, her regular, a hard time anyway."

I shrug, trying to act like this personal care stuff is no big deal. The thing is, it weirds me out. Brushing teeth, helping with dressing, cleaning fish tanks, that's all okay. But baths and showers? Well, that's just a bit too personal.

Mrs. Buckley flashes me a sly smile as I enter her apartment. "Derek. You came back.

That's lovely." She beckons me to come closer. "That girl Paula, she was always bossing me around. Treating me like a child."

I nod.

"I'm eighty-six years old," she says. "I'm not a child."

"No. No, you're not."

She looks sideways at me. "You won't try to boss me, will you, Derek?"

I shake my head. "No, ma'am." I've never called anyone Ma'am before in my life. I have no idea why I just said that.

Mrs. Buckley smiles again. "I don't need a bath this morning," she says.

"Francine said…" I begin.

She gives a little sniff. "Francine. Puffed-up little git. What does she know?"

I shrug helplessly.

"I had a bath yesterday," Mrs. Buckley says. "Today I'm going to show you some photos."

I spend the next hour looking at pictures of Mrs. Buckley's life. A small child posed serious-faced with groups of adults. A bride and groom standing hand in hand. A mother with a pair of toddlers clinging to her legs. A cute dark-haired baby sitting on Santa's lap. An older couple on the deck of a sailboat. That one reminds me of Aaliyah and I shiver a little.

Mrs. Buckley's sharp eyes don't miss much. "Goose walking over your grave?"

I shake my head. "Just cold."

"Hmm." She looks at the clock. "You better go. Francine doesn't like it when the care workers overstay their time."

I look at my watch. Crap. I'm really late. I nod thanks to Mrs. Buckley and run down the stairs, practically knocking over an old man at the bottom.

Francine is sitting behind her desk, drinking coffee. She shoots a sharp glance at me. "Mrs. Buckley give you any trouble?"

I shake my head, deciding not to mention that I didn't give her a bath.

Francine taps her watch but doesn't say anything, just gives me a list of appointments for the day. To my relief, Aaliyah's name isn't on it. Just thinking about yesterday makes my cheeks and neck burn. I don't know what I was thinking, going to talk to her like that.

Chapter Seven

After work, I lie on my bed and stare at the ceiling, thinking. Weird things are getting to me lately. Take Aaliyah, for example. And now old Mrs. Buckley and her photographs. They keep popping into my head for no reason. It's so strange that someone can be young and have a family and do all those things and then end up all alone, stuck in a lousy little apartment with bossy care workers and a bunch of old pictures. It's depressing.

I don't want that to be me.

I pick up the phone and call Gabi. She's my best friend, I guess. We don't see each other all that often, but we've been friends forever and she's one of the few people I really talk about things with.

She picks up on the first ring. "Yellow?"

"That's so corny, that *yellow* thing. I wish you'd drop it already."

She laughs. "Let me guess. My cheerful and always supportive friend Derek."

"Ha ha." I clear my throat. "What are you doing tonight?"

"Got a date. Getting together with that barista from Java Joe's. You know, the tall girl with the black hair? The really, really cute one with the eyebrow ring and the gorgeous smile?"

"Uh-huh." Gabi, unlike me, seems to have no difficulty finding dates. Even the straight girls have crushes on her.

"What's up, Derek?"

I try to sound casual. "Nothing major. Just be good to talk to you, that's all."

"Uh-huh. Cut the crap and tell me what's going on."

The thing is, I'm having some trouble talking. There seems to be a golf ball lodged in my throat and it hurts to swallow. *Get a grip, you freaking idiot.*

"Gabi," I say. My voice cracks embarrassingly.

"It's your dad, isn't it? Is he drunk? What happened?" Gabi's voice rises. "Should I come over?"

"No. He's fine. Well, you know. The usual. He's passed out on the couch with the television blaring." I pause, listening. From the living room, I can hear some reality show host encouraging the contestants to eat cockroaches.

There's a long pause.

"Derek...I can cancel this date if you want."

"Nah, don't do that."

"Tomorrow, then."

Across my bedroom, the computer screen is black and empty. This is the first time in months that I haven't checked my messages the second I walked in the door.

"Okay," I say. "Tomorrow night. Java

Joe's? Or will you be too busy flirting with your barista if we go there?"

I can picture Gabi nodding, grinning.

"She's not working tomorrow night," she says. "See you there."

That night, for the first time since I met Ethan, I don't even turn on my computer. I look at his picture about a hundred times though: that smile, those eyes. Instead of that giddy warm feeling I usually get when I look at him, now I just feel cold and sick.

I can't believe I could've been so stupid as to think this could ever work.

Francine greets me with her tight smile the next morning. "You're seeing Mrs. Buckley first," she says. "Basic cleaning. She's been hiding food again."

I nod. "Okay."

"Then Aaliyah. She needs help getting ready for a lunch date."

"A lunch date?"

"She's expecting you by 10 AM. If you

have time in between, we're still short-staffed in the kitchen."

"She doesn't like male care workers," I say.

Francine looks at me oddly. "Well, she asked for you."

I'm pretty nervous, to be honest. Something about Aaliyah really gets to me. Plus I made such an ass of myself last time I saw her. I shake my head and try to push the memory aside.

Mrs. Buckley is happy to see me, anyway. She pats her white curly hair and smiles at me as if she's invited me round for breakfast. I wish I could just drink tea and let her talk, but instead I tell her that we're supposed to be cleaning up the hidden food.

The smile falls away and her face crumples. "Derek. I thought you understood."

I shake my head. "Not really."

She turns her back and pretends to read a magazine. I clean up in silence, feeling like a traitor.

At ten o'clock sharp, I knock on Aaliyah's door.

"So," she says.

I look at my running shoes, which are new and too white. "Francine said you need to get ready for a lunch date."

She nods. "I do, but I don't need much help. Just fixing my hair so it looks decent."

You wouldn't know it from what you see on TV, but being gay actually does not automatically mean a guy is a good hairdresser.

I gesture to my own shaggy hair. "Hair's not really one of my skills, you know."

Aaliyah laughs. "That's okay. I just need it brushed and tied back." She makes a face. "I should just get it cut short. Then I could manage it myself."

"That makes sense."

"I don't know why I haven't done it yet." She pauses, looks at me and makes a face. "Yes I do. It's like giving up, you know? Saying I'm not going to get better."

"It would grow again," I say. I'm still

really curious about what's wrong with her, but I know better than to ask.

Aaliyah laughs again, but this time it sounds like she's laughing at me. She wheels her chair over to a table and picks up a hairbrush. "Here."

I take the brush and move behind her. "Just brush it?"

"Yeah."

"So," I ask casually, "what's your lunch date?"

"My ex-fiancé," she says.

I'm dying to ask questions but I just keep brushing her hair.

"Did Francine tell you I asked for you?" she asks.

"Uh-huh."

She is quiet for a minute. Then she speaks softly. "How old are you?"

I hesitate. "Seventeen. But Francine thinks I'm twenty."

"Francine's a stupid cow," she says.

"That's harsh."

Aaliyah shrugs, pulling her hair away. "Ow." She twists in the wheelchair to look at me. "She is though. This place sucks."

I don't say anything. It does suck.

"Anyway," she says, "I asked for you because I felt bad about what I said last time. You know. About you just wanting to hear that I did something stupid, that it was my fault."

I nod and force myself to meet her eyes. "You were right," I admit. "Anyway, it's none of my business."

"I had an aneurysm," she says abruptly. "A blood vessel just blew in my head. No warning, no reason. Just—pow. One minute I was planning my wedding and working on a master's degree. Next thing I knew I was in hospital and couldn't even go to the bathroom without help."

I wince. "Wow. That's pretty intense." *Wow*? *Intense?* Could I say something more stupid?

She laughs. "Indeed."

"But you're having lunch with your fiancé," I blunder on. "I mean, that's good, right?"

She turns her head away, signalling me to finish brushing her hair. "He won't stop calling," she says. "I finally agreed to meet him one last time. Maybe he needs to hear in person that it's over."

"*You* ended it?" I blurt out.

"Yes. You assumed he did, right?"

"I don't know," I say, trying to backpedal. "I just thought, maybe…"

"Sure. Maybe no one would want to be with someone like me, right?" Aaliyah spits the words out. "Guess what, Derek? No one would."

"But you ended it?"

She nods and I stop brushing. "I don't want him sticking around out of pity," she says. "I don't need that."

I'm silent for a moment. "You're still the same person, though," I say. "I mean, he wouldn't just stop caring about you."

Aaliyah wheels herself forward and turns to face me. "I don't want to be 'cared about'," she says.

I hold up a green hair tie that is twisted around the handle of her hairbrush. "You want this on?"

She shrugs. "I guess it seems kind of weird, me trying to look good when I'm just ending the relationship anyway."

I think about Ethan for a moment.

"No," I say. "Not so weird."

Chapter Eight

Sometimes I really wish I could call Mom. Like I said, I don't blame her for leaving Dad, but I wish she could have found a way to leave him without leaving me too. Or I wish she'd left years ago and taken me with her. I guess she tried once, when I was a kid. We stayed in a women's shelter. It was okay. There were some other kids and the counselors were nice. We didn't stay long though. Mom said she wasn't like the other women there, that Dad wasn't as bad as all that.

The weird thing is, it used to seem like she wasn't very strong—like Dad was twice as big and twice as loud. But since Mom left, he's kind of shriveled up and faded away.

And I'm twice as big as him now. He doesn't scare me anymore. But I think I'll always hate him for driving Mom away.

When I get home from work, he's sitting on the couch as usual, with the TV on. It's some news show. A gay couple in Vancouver has just won some court case.

"Look at this crap," Dad says, gesturing with the remote control. "Gays getting married, wanting this and that. God created Adam and Eve, not—"

"Adam and Steve," I say wearily. "I know, Dad."

He looks at me suspiciously. "I'm not a bigot, if that's what you're thinking," he says. "People can do what they want in private. I just don't see why they have to drag everyone else into their business."

If there is one thing I know for sure, it is that trying to reason with my father is a complete and utter waste of time. I try anyway. "Straight people don't have to keep their lives and marriages and relationships private."

He stares at me like I'm the idiot. "Sounds like the kind of bleeding-heart crap your mother always says."

"Mom's gone," I say. "Remember?" Then I walk past him to my room.

Ethan's not online but there's an e-mail from him in my inbox:

> *hey derek. i didn't hear from you yesterday, hope everything is okay. my sister is here for a visit and now everyone is all obsessed with this wedding—all they talk about is flowers and cakes and bridesmaids' dresses. it's kind of funny. they think i'm excited about it too—and i am, only it's seeing you that i'm excited about, not the wedding itself.*
>
> *tho actually it is kind of cool, seeing my sister all blissed out about this guy and planning a life with him. made me wonder if I'll ever do that.*

you think you would? get married, i
mean? (don't panic. not a proposal!
just curious)

I hit *reply* and start typing:

hey ethan.

Then I freeze up. I want to tell him about what my dad just said about gay marriage, and about Aaliyah and Mrs. Buckley…to tell him about everything, the way I have been for the last few months. But how can I keep talking to him like nothing is wrong? And how do I end this without hurting him?

In the end, I just switch off the computer and lie on my bed until it's time to meet Gabi.

Gabi's already at Java Joe's when I arrive, her hair all spiked up and newly blond.

"Hey, babe," she says.

"Hey, Gabi." I slide into the chair across from her. "Nice hair."

"I already ordered," she says.

Two frothy, pale green, whipped-cream-topped drinks are sitting on the table.

I grimace. "What is that?"

"Mint mocha latte," she says. "It's on me."

Gabi never drinks regular coffee like everyone else. She likes her drinks sugar-filled. She doesn't usually make me drink them though.

"What's up?" I ask. "Why the generosity with the frothy green beverages?"

She grins. "We're celebrating."

"Ah. Last night was a success then?"

She leans across the table and grabs my arm. "Derek, success would be an understatement."

I raise one eyebrow. "You got laid?"

"So crude," Gabi says, pretending to be shocked. Then she winks. "She is so hot."

"And not so straight?"

Gabi grins broadly. "Not so straight at all."

This is Gabi's solution to living in a small town. As she says, she's already dated all the girls who know they're queer. Now she's dating the ones who aren't quite sure.

She suddenly turns serious. "What about you, Derek? What's up?"

I frown. "It's Ethan."

"No way. He didn't dump you. I don't believe it."

Gabi's heard a lot about Ethan over the past few months. She's even read some of his e-mails.

"No," I say, hesitating. I have to talk to someone but it feels so…humiliating.

"What is it then?" Her pixie face creases with concern, and her green eyes meet mine.

"Ethan is flying out from BC," I say. "His sister's getting married in Kitchener and he wants to come and see me."

Gabi stares at me. "And? Hello? This is a problem because?"

I shake my head. "This is really embarrassing."

"You're shy." She tilts her head to one side. "He doesn't know he's your first, you know, boyfriend?"

"It's not that. He knows that."

"So what's the problem?"

I take a sip of sugary whipped cream. "Ugh," I say.

"Derek. Come on. What's wrong?"

I stare at the surface of my drink and stir it with the spoon. "I sent him a picture of myself. An old one. You know, before I put on all this weight."

Gabi looks surprised. "You did? Why?"

"Yeah. I know it was stupid but I didn't really think we'd ever meet, you know?"

She studies my face. "It's not that big a deal. So you're a bit heavier than you were. You're still the same person he's been talking to every day for months. For, like, hours. And hours and hours—"

"I'm not going to meet him. I can't."

Gabi grabs her spiky hair with both hands. "Derek! Don't be an idiot. This guy is the best thing that's happened to you in ages."

"Thanks."

"Seriously. You and Ethan are—I don't know, soul mates or something. You're crazy about him. He's crazy about you."

I blink. "I know."

"So what are you going to do?"

"I'm going to break up with him," I say. "I have to."

She shakes her head. "No. No, no, no. Don't do that. You guys are really good together."

"Gabi, we've never met. I'm not letting him come all the way out here so he can dump me in person when he finds out I'm fat."

"You're not."

I just look at her.

She shrugs. "Okay, so you're fat. You're also terrific, smart, funny and kind. And you're still the same person Ethan fell in love with. Give the guy a chance."

I fold my arms across my chest. Maybe Gabi is right. Maybe Ethan would be able to see past the fat.

But I've already made up my mind.

Chapter Nine

I figure there's no point in putting it off. So when I get home, I switch on the computer. Ethan's not online, which is good. I don't think I could handle a conversation about this.

> *ethan*, I write, *i've been thinking about things and i think it would be better if u didn't come here. i don't think we should meet in person. the thing is, i don't think we should really continue this relationship. i'm sorry. i hope*

u have a good time at the wedding anyway.

I rub my hands over my face. I feel like I should say more, give some explanation, but there's no explanation I can give. I delete the last line, the one about having a good time at the wedding. Then I hit send.

At 3 AM I'm still awake, wondering what Ethan will think when he reads the e-mail. I roll over and kick off the blankets. Too hot, too cold, too hot. Finally I get out of bed, find Ethan's picture under the mouse pad and take it back to bed with me. I turn on my bedside light and study the face: his easy smile, his smooth cheeks and straight nose, his warm brown eyes. I trace the smile with my finger, lay the picture beside me on my pillow and turn out the light.

It seems like a few minutes later that my alarm is going off. I drag myself out of bed, brush my teeth, gargle with mouthwash. I keep looking at the computer while I'm getting dressed. Ethan will still be sleeping, since it's three hours earlier out west.

Francine tells me I'm with Aaliyah again this morning. As I walk up the stairs, I realize I'm glad. She's prickly as hell, but there's something about her.

She's waiting in the living room, her hair lank and dark gray shadows ringing her eyes.

"I need a shower," she says.

"Okay." I look at her. "I thought you didn't like male care workers."

She shrugs. "You're okay. Besides, that girl Paula makes me crazy. Talks to me like I'm retarded, or six years old. Like this place is a daycare for toddlers."

I grin. "That's what Mrs. Buckley says too."

"The old lady down the hall?" Aaliyah looks surprised.

"Yeah. She's all right. You should talk to her sometime. I think she gets lonely."

"Well, aren't you just Mr. Sensitive," Aaliyah says, wheeling herself into the bathroom.

I follow her in. "Ready to go?"

She nods and I start unbuttoning her

shirt. "So," I say, "what happened with your ex? Did you tell him you wanted to end it?"

"I did." She meets my eyes for a second. Then she drops her gaze.

"Umm…how did you tell him? What did he say?" I picture Ethan sitting in front of his computer, reading my words.

She shrugs, helping me slide the shirt off. "Just said I didn't want to see him anymore and asked him to stop calling."

"You don't seem…well, it's none of my business, but you don't look so good."

"You're right. It's none of your business."

I turn on the taps and hold my hand under the water, testing the temperature.

Aaliyah stares at me. "You don't look so hot yourself."

"That's hardly news," I say.

"Ha ha." She studies my face. "Are you seeing anyone?"

I ignore the question. I help her up and out of her pants.

When she is sitting under the running

water, she asks me again. "Well? Do you have a girlfriend?"

I shake my head, but to my surprise I find myself telling her anyway. "I was seeing someone," I say. "Online. You know. A long-distance thing."

She raises her eyebrows. "And?"

"And nothing. We broke up. I...I actually just broke it off last night."

It sounds so strange, hearing myself say it out loud. Right this minute, I'd give anything to reach out into cyberspace and snatch back that e-mail. Just as well I can't, I guess. I look at myself in the bathroom mirror. E-mail is one thing, but I can't imagine Ethan loving this body in person. And it's not like I can lose eighty pounds in a few months.

Aaliyah is watching me, water streaming down her back and shoulders. Her dark eyes are thoughtful. "Why did you end it?"

I shrug and look away. "Just wasn't working out." I reach for the shampoo and start washing her hair.

When I get home, Dad is waiting for me. In his hand is Ethan's picture.

"Uh, hi?" I say tentatively.

He doesn't waste any time. "Who is this? I found it on your pillow."

"What were you doing in my room? Snooping around?"

He stares at me, jaw tight. "Just answer the question."

For the second time today, I find myself saying more than I intended to. "His name's Ethan."

"And? What the hell is this…Ethan's… picture doing on your pillow?"

To tell the truth, I'm pretty taken aback. I know Dad snoops—that's nothing new. He likes to control every little thing, which means he has to know every little thing. It was one of the things that made Mom crazy. He used to go through her purse and her date-book, stuff like that. But his reaction to this photograph? It makes me wonder if he's been suspecting something for a while.

I'm just staring at him, trying to decide what to say. His face is getting redder and redder, and a little muscle in his jaw is popping out, twitching around.

"Dad?" I hesitate.

I've never wanted to come out to my dad. I'd have told Mom, if she'd stuck around, but I know Dad will freak. But Ethan's face is flickering in my mind, and I refuse to let my father go on bullying me. I refuse to lie about the best thing that's ever happened to me.

Even now that it's over.

"His name is Ethan," I say again. "We were seeing each other. He was my boyfriend."

I'm bracing myself, not sure if he's going to hit me or throw something or just start shouting. But he doesn't say anything. He just looks away from me. He stares out the window, not saying a word.

The clock is ticking loudly. My heart is racing and my shirt is soaked with sweat. It seems like ten minutes go by but maybe it's only two.

"Dad?"

He slowly turns back to me and his face is stiff and cold. "I'm going out," he says.

"I want you and your stuff gone by the time I get back."

He rips the picture of Ethan in half and lets the two torn pieces fall to the floor.

Chapter Ten

I stuff some clothes into a backpack. I have no idea what to do but I'm not sticking around. For a second I look at the computer and imagine telling Ethan about what just happened. There's a weird empty ache in my gut whenever I think about him.

So don't think about him, I tell myself. *Think about what to do.*

I cram a few CD's into my backpack. I can't possibly pack up all my stuff now. I'll have to get boxes and come back. Where would I put it all, anyway? My car? I don't even know where I'm going.

One thing I do know is that I don't want to be here when Dad gets back. Right now I don't care if I never see him again. Don't get me wrong—if he decides to apologize, I'll listen. I can't see it happening though. Dad has never said he's sorry for any of the things he's done. I don't think he knows how. I sling my backpack over my shoulder and head out.

On the living room floor, something catches my eye. The torn pieces of Ethan's picture, just lying there where Dad dropped them. I hesitate, and then I pick them up. I should just drop them in the garbage, but I can't quite do it. Instead, my hand slides the ripped-up picture into my pocket.

For a moment I wonder if I should try to find Mom somehow. I have this kind of romantic image of myself hitchhiking down to California. But I wouldn't know where to start. How many religious cults are there in California? Probably hundreds. And it's not like they'd be listed in the phone book.

Besides, Mom walked out. So screw that idea.

I pick up the phone and call Gabi. "Can I crash at your place? Dad…well, I guess he's kicked me out."

"Bastard," Gabi says. "What happened?"

"I told him about Ethan."

"No way."

"Way."

Gabi whistles softly. "You're a crazy man, Derek. What'd you do that for?"

I'm quiet for a minute. "To tell you the truth, I don't know. I wasn't planning on it. Besides, I already broke up with Ethan anyway."

"You didn't!"

"I did. I'll fill you in later, okay?"

Gabi is still talking when I put the phone down.

Gabi's parents are great. They don't ask any questions. They just say that the spare room is mine for as long as I need it. You can tell they mean it and that they're not just being polite. Her house has always been like that, ever since we were little kids: kind of open and welcoming, with lots of people in and out, cooking and listening to music and arguing about books and ideas.

They're even cool with Gabi being a dyke. Lots of their friends are gay. They probably have no idea how much difference that has made to me, just seeing that not everyone is like my own family. That there are other ways to be in the world. That there are choices.

Gabi's new girlfriend, the one from Java Joe's, shows up right after I get there. It's kind of a relief, to be honest. If I was alone with Gabi, I know she'd have a thousand questions, and really, all I want to do is go to bed.

In the spare room, I put the torn halves of Ethan's picture on the dresser, carefully lined up. Then I lie on the bed, thinking about him. I wonder if he's e-mailed me. I wonder what he said. I hope…I don't know. That he's not too hurt. That he doesn't hate me for doing this.

Ethan. Mom. Dad. It's all too freaking much. I imagine my life stretching out ahead of me, a long, endless empty ache. I rummage through my stuff, looking for something to eat, and find a bag of chocolate chip cookies

I took from home. I'm just about to rip it open when I remember old Mrs. Buckley, hiding bits of food in her room. And I think about Dad and his drinking, and Mom and her religious cult. All these ways people get through the days. I stare at the bag for a minute. Then I toss it into the garbage and crawl back into bed. Hot tears sneak out of my eyes and run silently into my hair.

"Quit feeling sorry for yourself," I whisper. But I can't. I can't.

The next day, I head off to work as usual.

Francine pounces on me the minute I walk through the front door.

"Derek, can you come into my office, please?"

My heart quickens. My first thought is that she's going to fire me, but I haven't really done anything wrong that I can think of. I sit down and Francine takes her seat behind the big desk. Her face is tight and hard to read. I find myself thinking of Aaliyah. Has something happened to her? Another aneurysm? Can that happen?

But it's something else entirely.

Chapter Eleven

Francine taps her long fingernails on the desk. They're painted a pale shade of purple and look like Halloween. "Aaliyah's asked for you again," she says.

I nod, relieved. "Okay."

She shakes her head, lips thin and tight. "Derek, if there's something going on, I need you to tell me. Right now."

"What do you mean?"

"I think you know what I mean."

I don't have a clue, so I just sit there

staring at her. Has she found out that I lied on my resume or something?

She sighs. "I'm not stupid, Derek. All these months of insisting on no male caregivers, and now she's requesting you every day?"

The pieces finally click into place. I almost laugh. "You mean…you think Aaliyah and I…No. No. Nothing like that."

She just sits there. Flint-eyed. Unbelieving.

"She's not my type," I say stupidly.

Francine sighs again. "Well, I can't force you to admit anything, but I'm assigning Paula to Aaliyah for the time being."

Aaliyah hates Paula. I don't say anything but I feel like the room just got ten degrees hotter.

"Mrs. Buckley, then?" I ask. My voice sounds flat.

Francine shakes her head. "She was admitted to hospital last night. Chest infection. Not good at her age." She shrugs. "Well, there's plenty of names on the wait list."

I help a couple of older men get dressed. Then I clean up an empty apartment. I don't know who lived here, don't know whether they moved out or died. There are some photos taped to the wall and I leave them in a neat pile on the counter, thinking about Mrs. Buckley.

On my lunch break, I sneak upstairs to see Aaliyah. I know this is stupid, but I don't want her to think it's my choice not to see her anymore.

"So what's up?" I ask her.

She looks at me. "You look like crap, Derek. No offence."

I laugh but it sounds flat and hollow even to my own ears. "None taken."

"So where were you this morning? I got stuck with Paula the day-care lady."

There's a long silence and I force myself to meet her eyes. "Aaliyah, Francine said you asked for me and I didn't know if she was going to tell you…"

"Tell me what?"

"She's taken me off the schedule for you, for a while anyway." I shrug an apology. "I'm sorry. I didn't want you to think it was my choice."

Aaliyah closes her eyes for a second. "My fault," she says.

"Huh?"

"I should've gone on saying I didn't want male caregivers."

I feel my cheeks getting warm, but I figure she should have all the information. "She thinks we're, you know…involved."

She just snorts. "She doesn't really think that. You're just a kid."

"I'm not," I protest.

Aaliyah looks at me, eyes dark. "Francine just loves her power. This is the kind of thing she does. This is why it's better never to let anyone know what you want. Better to pretend you don't care."

"Maybe if you told her? You know, that there's nothing going on with us?" For some reason, I really want Aaliyah to do this. Not just so I can keep seeing her, though I want that too.

It's because I want her to stand up for herself. To see that she has choices.

"Won't make a difference. Better to pretend you don't care," she says again. A muscle in her jaw twitches.

I shake my head helplessly. I feel like this is my fault somehow. "I'm sorry."

She laughs, sort of. A flat, totally unfunny laugh. "You're not so good at that, are you? Pretending not to care?"

I shrug, embarrassed. "I'd better get out of here. If Francine catches me, she'll really think something is going on."

Aaliyah grabs my sleeve. "Hang on. What's wrong with you, anyway?" Her eyes lock on mine and don't let go. "You're not just upset about Francine, are you?"

I shake my head.

"You miss your girlfriend?"

For a second I can't think what she's talking about.

"Your online relationship?" she prompts. "You said you ended it."

"Oh. It wasn't a girlfriend, it was a guy." I don't really care what she thinks right now. "I'm gay."

I watch her face carefully. She looks mildly

surprised but not shocked. Not upset. "Sorry. I shouldn't have assumed anything."

"S'okay."

"So. Is that what's wrong? You miss him?"

I shake my head. Then I change my mind and nod. "I miss him like crazy."

Next thing I know, all this emotion is rushing up inside me, crazy waves of feeling that knock me down and suck me under. I can't breathe properly and I'm about to start crying like a baby.

I mutter something, anything, pull my arm away from her and duck into the bathroom.

When I come back out, I've calmed myself down. "Sorry."

"What for?"

"You know. Unloading all that on you."

She grins a little but her eyes are sad. "It's okay. Makes a nice change, not just to be seen as someone who needs to be taken care of."

"That's not how I see you," I say. The words are automatic, but I realize I mean it. "I like talking to you. I do." I watch her face carefully, hoping she won't get all prickly again.

She looks solemn but not at all mad. "So tell me why you dumped your boyfriend then."

I shake my head. "It's really personal. Embarrassing."

Aaliyah snorts. "Please. Needing help to take a shower? That's personal."

I can see the rain streaming down outside the window. I guess it must be setting that record by now. I watch the cars going in and out of the parking lot and listen to the clock ticking loudly in the apartment.

Aaliyah just waits.

"I really like this guy a lot," I said. My voice sounds low and choky, and I clear my throat.

"So why did you end it?" Aaliyah asks. Her eyebrows are pulled together in a puzzled frown.

"He was going to visit," I say slowly, watching her face. "The thing is, I haven't always been like this. I haven't always been fat. And, uh, I sent him an old picture."

Aaliyah's frown clears and an expression I can't read takes its place. "You mean you're dumping him so he won't find out you're fat?"

I squirm inwardly. She makes it sound so pathetic. "Yeah," I say. "Basically."

"That is seriously the stupidest thing I've ever heard." She wheels her chair a little closer to me and looks at me straight on.

I can't meet her eyes.

"You guys have been talking online, right? I mean, you know each other from conversations. It's not like he fell for you because of how you look."

I shake my head. "I guess not. I mean, no. We didn't even exchange photos until we'd been talking for a few months."

"So don't you think you should give the guy some credit?"

"What do you mean?"

"I mean, maybe he's not totally shallow. Maybe he might care about more than whether your body is perfect or not. Maybe you should give him a chance."

Aaliyah is leaning toward me, her dark eyes intense.

"I don't think so," I say. "I don't really need the humiliation of getting dumped in person."

She bangs her fist awkwardly on the arm of her chair. "Don't be a coward."

"Excuse me," I say. "I don't think you get to call me a coward. Not after you just dumped your boyfriend for the same reason."

Her eyes are daggers. "It's not the same," she says, spitting the words out.

"Your body's not perfect. Neither is mine. So what's the difference? If I'm a coward, so are you."

"You don't understand anything," she says.

Impulsively, I put my hand on her arm. "Maybe I understand more than you think."

Aaliyah stares at me for a long minute, and I can see her dark eyes starting to shine with tears. She blinks them away and puts her hand over mine.

"Maybe you do," she says, so softly that I have to lean close to hear her. "Maybe we're both cowards."

Chapter Twelve

As I wipe clean the tables in the dining room, I can't stop thinking about Aaliyah's words. Am I a coward?

Duh. Obviously. But if I think she should give her fiancé a chance—if I think he deserves a chance—then doesn't Ethan deserve one too?

It sounds good in theory. If this was happening to someone else—like Aaliyah, say—I know what my advice would be.

But when I imagine actually meeting

Ethan, all I can see is the disappointment on his face when he sees what I look like now. "You lied to me," I imagine him saying. I realize that I've never even heard his voice. I watch my wet cloth making smeary circles on the table and feel kind of dizzy. Is it possible to be dizzy from missing someone? More likely it's just that I've forgotten to eat all day.

"Derek?"

I look up. "Mrs. Buckley?"

She's back, leaning on her walker, wearing a blue tracksuit with a thick white housecoat over top and looking around the dining room like she owns it.

"I heard you were sick," I say. "I guess you're better?"

Mrs. Buckley cackles with laughter. "Of course I am," she says. "I wasn't going to hang around that hospital any longer than I had to. One night was plenty." She leans closer to me. "The nurses were terrible," she says. "They kept taking my food away before I'd finished with it. Wouldn't even let me save a few bites for later."

I remember the moldy bagels hidden in her dresser drawers and can't help smiling. "That's too bad," I say.

She smiles back at me. "My grandson came to bring me home. And at least it's finally stopped raining."

I turn and look out the window. I hadn't noticed, but she's right. The clouds have parted to reveal a sky such a pale shade of blue that it looks like it's been bleached clean by the rain.

"Everything okay, Gran?" A guy has stepped into the room behind her. He takes her arm protectively.

I do a double take. He is seriously good-looking. Dark hair and eyes, long lean muscles, blue jeans that fit like they cost a lot of money. "You're her grandson?" I ask stupidly.

"Uh-huh. And you're Derek. I've heard all about you."

"You have?"

"Oh yeah. Gran says she showed you my baby pictures." He grins widely, showing straight white teeth. "She said you thought I was cute."

I blush furiously. Is he flirting with me? I look at Mrs. Buckley, who is nodding happily, and figure out what he's talking about. "Oh. The baby with Santa."

He nods and holds out his hand. "I'm Keenan."

I shake his hand. "Nice to meet you."

He grins again. "Thanks for taking care of my gran. She's pretty special, huh?"

"Yeah. Yeah, she is."

He guides Mrs. Buckley toward the door. Then he turns back to me. "Maybe I'll see you around," he says, winking.

I manage to smile but to tell you the truth, I'm kind of stunned. Keenan is seriously hot, and I'm 95 percent certain that he was flirting with me. For a second I feel really, really good. I turn toward the window. Even through the glass, I think I can feel the warmth of that high winter-white sun.

Then a wave of longing hits me like a brick wall, and all I can see in my mind is Ethan's face.

God, I miss him.

Gabi and I make a huge pot of vegetarian chili. After eating dinner with her folks, we head down to Java Joe's. I need to go by Dad's place tonight to get my stuff, but I'm putting it off. I really don't want to see my father.

It's clear and cold outside and Java Joe's is busy. Music is playing loudly and the windows are all steamed up. It's my turn to buy: regular coffee for me and something strawberry flavored and frothy for Gabi.

"Do you think I'm a coward?" I ask her when we're sitting at our favorite corner table.

She looks surprised. "Of course not. Why?"

"I met this woman," I say slowly.

Gabi opens her eyes wide. "Derek! You're kidding!"

I make a face at her. "Please. Not like that. She's a friend. Well, a client I guess. She's one of the residents at the place I work."

She looks curious. "Okay."

I take a sip of my coffee. "Well, she said I was a coward for dumping Ethan. For not at least trying, you know? Not giving him a chance."

"That's a bit harsh," Gabi says.

I make a face: half grin, half grimace. "She says it like it is, you know? She doesn't pull any punches."

Gabi looks at me, head tilted to one side. "What do you think?"

The radio is playing some old love song. I put my elbows on the table and rest my chin on my hands. "I think she might be right."

"So?"

I avoid her eyes. "So nothing. So I'm a coward."

"Derek! You can't just give up. It's too important to you." Gabi's practically jumping off her seat in frustration.

I shrug. "It's not that big a deal."

Aaliyah's right. It's way easier just to pretend you don't care.

Chapter Thirteen

It's almost ten o'clock when Gabi taps her watch, tilts her head to one side and says, "Well?"

"Yeah. I should get moving." I make a face. "I just don't feel like dealing with my dad tonight, you know?"

"Can't say I blame you. Still, you have to get your stuff sometime."

She's right. I don't know what I was thinking when I packed, but I've got nothing decent to wear to work tomorrow. "If I'm lucky, he'll be asleep on the couch."

"If we're going, let's do it," Gabi says as she gets up.

"If *we're* going?"

"I'm coming with you."

"Gabi." I look up at her for a long moment. "You let me stay at your place, you listen to me and let me dump all this crap on you... You're the best. If we were even slightly straight, I'd ask you to marry me."

She laughs. "Yeah, yeah."

I push my chair back and get to my feet slowly. "You know what though? I think I need to do this on my own."

The lights are all still on when I get to my dad's place. My place until last night, but already it doesn't feel like home. The truth is it hasn't felt much like home since Mom left.

I hesitate at the door, wondering whether I'm supposed to knock. It's tempting just to walk in. If Dad's passed out, I might be able to sneak past and grab my stuff without having to say a word. On the other hand, Dad made it pretty clear that I'm no longer welcome here.

I knock loudly. Then I wait. My heart bangs around, *thump thump thump*, all fast and hard and uneven, like it's lost its rhythm. Finally I hear footsteps, and then the door swings open.

Dad stands there, hand on the door knob, not saying anything. He's wearing saggy burgundy sweatpants and a white T-shirt that's a size too small.

"I've come to pack up my stuff," I tell him.

He steps backward to let me in and then closes the door behind me. I don't take my shoes off, although this is one of the many things Dad has big control issues about. I just walk right past him down the hallway to my bedroom.

What used to be my bedroom.

Dad has dumped all the clothes from my closet, all the books from my shelf, all my stuff, in one jumbled heap on the floor. I don't say anything. I just start packing. Socks, photo albums, sweaters, school yearbooks, winter coat, pack of markers—I don't sort it out. I just cram it all into my backpack and the extra bags I brought.

I can feel Dad standing there, in the hallway behind me, watching. His eyes are burning holes in my back but I don't turn around. I just keep packing, keep breathing, keep telling myself it's just a few more minutes until I'm out of here.

Dad clears his throat. "Derek."

I don't answer. The only thing he could say that I'd want to hear is *sorry*.

"Look," he says. His voice is cracked and high-pitched. He doesn't sound like himself at all. Despite my intentions, I turn around and look at him. Those skinny legs and that sticking-out stomach, those track pants pulled halfway up to his armpits.

"Look," he says again. "This isn't how I expected things to be." His face crumples. He looks lost. He looks *old*. "This isn't how it was all supposed to turn out," he says.

"Yeah, well." I start to turn away, to pick up the next armful of crap to stuff into a bag.

"I just want you to know that," he says. "I didn't choose this."

"You think I did?" It comes out in a weird croak, and to cover up I raise my voice so that I'm practically yelling. "I haven't had a whole lot of choices either, Dad."

There's a long, long silence.

"This gay thing," he starts to say.

I cut him off. "You know what? I'm not really interested in discussing *this gay thing,* as you call it."

He sighs and folds his arms across his chest. "Your mom would know how to handle this."

He just doesn't get it. "Mom's gone," I tell him. "She's gone. When are you going to get it through your head that she's not coming back?"

Dad stares at me. His face is pale and he has dark baggy circles under his eyes. He looks like hell. I feel a flicker of pity and, beneath it, some crazy mixture of feelings, anger and sadness and I don't know what else, all bubbling up inside me and threatening to spill over.

I take a deep breath. "It's just us now, Dad," I say, more softly. "It's just you and me."

"I'm tired," he says. "I'm going to bed." He starts to turn away. Then he hesitates and looks back at me. "If you decide to forget about the gay thing, I guess you could move back in."

It's so stupid I almost laugh, except I feel more like crying. So I just nod and keep on packing.

Chapter Fourteen

After a few days of having me in the spare room, Gabi's folks ask if I'd like to stay with them more permanently. They've got a basement suite and they've been thinking about renting it out but don't really want a stranger living there.

The amount they want to charge me is ridiculously low. Pocket change. I know what they're doing. They don't want me to go back to my dad's place unless things between him and me change a whole lot, and they know me well enough to know that I'm starting to worry about overstaying my welcome. It's exactly the kind of thing that Gabi's parents would do.

I think it over for about three seconds before I accept.

Gabi's mom gives me a big hug. To her, I'm still the little kid who fell out of Gabi's tree fort in the second grade. She's still trying to put Band-Aids on my scraped knees.

I squirm away, but not too quickly. The truth is, her hugs feel pretty good.

Mom used to hug me like that. I usually try not to think about Mom, but the thought just pops into my mind. Maybe, I think, I will try to find her after all. Not hitchhike to California or anything too crazy, but just make some calls. You never know. Maybe I'll get lucky.

And maybe Dad will change.

But I'm not holding my breath. For now, I'm pretty happy to stay right here.

That night, my mind keeps drifting back to Aaliyah. It's bad enough to be stuck in a body that doesn't work the way it should, the way it used to. But to be stuck in another prison as well, with someone like Francine controlling every little thing about your life… The thought makes my stomach twist with angry frustration.

I can't sleep. Finally I get up and go to the computer. For once, I'm not thinking about Ethan.

A few minutes later I've found a web page for the local health authority. Residential programs, housing, assisted living. Program manager.

Francine's boss.

When I sneak up to see Aaliyah after my next shift, I tell her I've made a complaint about Francine. I don't know what reaction I expected, but it wasn't this.

"What the hell did you think you were doing?" she snaps, spitting the words out like they taste bad.

I step back, startled. "I just…I don't know. I just thought it wasn't right, the way she treats you."

Aaliyah's eyes are narrowed. "How she treats me is my business, not yours."

"It's my business too. Francine accused me of, you know, being involved with you."

She spins her chair around to look out the window. Her back is stiff, shoulders drawn up tightly, sharp prickles all over.

"Don't lie to me, Derek. That's not why you did it."

"Sure it is." I'm feeling a bit lost here. "I didn't mean to upset you." A little late, a thought occurs to me. "Will it…are you worried that it'll make things worse for you?"

She shakes her head. "No. Well, it couldn't really."

"Then why are you so mad about it?"

She spins back toward me. "Damn it, Derek. You were the one person here who at least treated me like an adult. Don't you think if I wanted to complain, I'd do it myself?"

"You didn't do it," I say, stung. "You were too busy pretending not to care."

"So? That's my choice. You don't have

to agree, but you have to let me make my own choices."

I stare at her. I can't think of anything to say. The thing is, she's right. I was feeling sorry for her. That's why I did it. Not because of what Francine accused me of. Not because I wanted to clear my name. But because I was feeling sorry for her.

"I'm sorry," I say at last. "I really am. I just…I just wanted to make one thing right. Just wanted to fix this one thing." My voice cracks a little and I shut up, swallow hard, dig my nails into my palms.

She finally sighs. "Try fixing your own life, not mine." The words are tough, but her voice is suddenly softer and I know she's not really mad anymore.

Or maybe she still is, a little, but she's willing to give me a break this time.

Aaliyah meets my eyes and smiles, her face relaxing. "I called him."

"Who?" But I know who she means as soon as the word is out of my mouth. "Your fiancé? You did? What happened?"

She looks a little embarrassed, almost

a little shy. "We're having dinner together tonight."

"You are?"

"Yeah." She laughs. "And I'm really nervous. I think…well, I think pretending not to care might have been easier."

"Yeah." I push Ethan out of my mind.

"Derek? He wants me to move in with him." Her eyes are wide. Scared? I can't tell.

"Wow." I'm happy for her, but I feel lonely all of a sudden. "I'll miss you, if you go."

"Well, I haven't decided anything yet. We'll talk about it over dinner." She gives me a crooked grin. "He's taking me to Shallot's."

Shallot's is probably the most expensive restaurant in town. Needless to say, I haven't been there. "Wow. That's pretty special."

"Yeah."

Something occurs to me. "Hey, Aaliyah? I'm not supposed to be here, really, but…well, my shift's over and, this dinner's a big deal." I look at her, not sure how she'll take this. "Can I help you get ready?"

Aaliyah hesitates. "Paula's coming."

I shrug. Pretending not to care.

She meets my eyes. "Screw Paula," she says. "Yeah. I'd love it if you'd help me get ready." She wheels her chair toward the bedroom, stops, turns and talks to me over her shoulder. "If Francine finds out, you'll be out on your ass."

I nod. "I think I'm pretty much done with this place anyway."

She raises one eyebrow.

"I was thinking, you know, about going back to school. Finishing grade twelve." I look down at my hands, missing the feel of the keyboard, missing the long late hours talking online. "Ethan was always bugging me to go back," I say. My voice seems to come from a long way away.

Aaliyah picks out the same soft brown shirt I helped her into the first time we met, with a straight denim skirt and brown nylons. Clumsy as always, I manage to snag one of her nylons and put a run in it. I expect her to snap at me, but she just laughs and tells me there's another pair in her drawer. I blow-dry and brush her hair so that it's straight and shining, help her put on blush and a touch of lipstick.

Of course, I don't know what I'm doing. But when we're done, she looks gorgeous.

She looks in the mirror. "Wow. You're good at this."

I shake my head. "Nah. It's just not that hard to make you look fabulous."

"So." She catches her lip between her teeth.

"So." I know it's none of my business but I ask anyway. "Do you think you'll say yes? You know, move in with him?"

Her eyes meet mine in the mirror. "I think I might."

I feel like giving her a hug, but she's not the huggy type. I touch her shoulder lightly, just for a second. "You're brave, Aaliyah."

She nods. "What about you? What are you going to do about that boyfriend of yours?"

I feel a weight settle inside me. "It might be too late," I say slowly. "It might be too late to change my mind."

She nods. "Mmm. And it might not."

Chapter Fifteen

Back at Gabi's, I stare at myself in the bathroom mirror. I splash cold water on my face, shave carefully, brush my teeth. I comb my hair and wish I'd had it cut more recently.

There is a soft knock on the door. "You're taking forever," Gabi hisses impatiently. "Come on."

I give my reflection one last look. *Okay*, I tell myself. *This is it. This is me. This is as good as it gets*. Then I follow Gabi down the hallway to her bedroom.

"Stand by the door," Gabi says.

I lean against the wall and try to look relaxed while Gabi adjusts the settings on her digital camera.

"Maybe I should check my e-mail first," I say. "What if he got my e-mail and hates me? What if there's a message from him saying he never wants to hear from me again?"

Gabi shrugs. "What if there is? Would you just leave it at that?"

I shake my head slowly. "I'd still owe him the truth."

"Well then." She lines up the camera. "Smile."

I do my best to stretch my mouth in an imitation of a smile and she clicks. The flash makes me blink.

Gabi looks at the picture. "Well, it's not your best picture ever."

I look at it anxiously. My eyes are half closed and the flash makes me look like a ghost.

"Maybe we should wait until the morning," Gabi says. "Flash pictures always look bad."

"Just take another," I say. "I'm not waiting until morning."

Gabi grins at me and lifts the camera again. "Okay. Try not to look like you're in front of a firing squad."

I lean back against the wall again. Tomorrow I'll quit the job. Then I'll go to visit Aaliyah, I think. Just as a friend, to find out how her dinner went. And I have to tell her about this. For some reason, the thought makes me smile.

The flash goes off.

"Got it!" Gabi says. She is studying the picture. "This looks more like you, Derek. See?"

I look at my own face in miniature on the tiny screen. "It'll do."

Gabi sits down at her computer, plugs in her camera and downloads the picture.

"Okay," she says, getting up again. "All set." She pats the chair, inviting me to sit down.

I sit.

"You nervous?"

"A bit. About saying it right, you know?

Explaining it all so that he might understand why I did it."

"Not about how he's going to respond?"

I think about it. "I can't do anything about that part."

"Yeah." She puts her hand on my shoulder. "But he'd better not be a jerk about it. That'd really piss me off."

I turn my head and look at her. "I'll be okay, you know. Really. Whatever happens." And it's funny, but as soon as I say it, I know it's true.

"Yeah. You will." She nods, her expression both surprised and thoughtful.

I turn back to the computer and rest my hands on the keyboard.

Gabi is still standing behind me, watching over my shoulder.

"Umm, Gabi?"

"Yeah?"

"Do you think I could…you know, get a little privacy?"

She puts her hands on my shoulders and squeezes. "Sorry. Of course you can. I'll crash on the couch in the den." She grins. "So you can take all the time you need."

After she's gone, I sit for a while just watching the screen saver, a goofy one with Santa's reindeer flying around the screen. I haven't checked my e-mail since I sent Ethan that awful note saying I wanted to end it. Not so long ago, I guess, but it feels like forever.

My heart is beating so fast.

Finally I punch in my password, and there in my inbox is a message from Ethan.

Subject: Not without a fight.

I open his message and read it.

> *derek. i know u said u didn't want to continue this but i can't accept that. not without some explanation. not without a fight.*
>
> *everything was great until i said i was coming out to Ontario. so tell me what's wrong. please.*
>
> *u know what i think? i think ur scared about meeting in person. u think i'm not? it scares the hell out of me. i'm scared u won't like me as much in person, i'm scared i won't know what to say, i'm scared i won't turn u on. i'm scared u will think i'm a lousy*

*kisser. seriously. i've actually worried
about that.*

*but now i'm just scared i'll never get
a chance to find out.*

I read it again and again and again. I take
a deep breath.

Then I start typing.

Robin Stevenson grew up in England and Ontario, and now lives in Victoria, British Columbia. She is the author of several novels for teens, including *Out of Order*, *Dead in the Water* and *Impossible Things*. More information about Robin is available on her website: www.robinstevenson.com.